JE

For Nick, the funniest, most handsome teacher our children ever had – M.F.

To my two super-awesome ladies, Allister and Katrin – M.L.

Text © 2013 Maureen Fergus
Illustrations © 2013 Mike Lowery

Kids Can Press acknowledges the financial support of the Government of Ontario, through the Ontario Media Development Corporation's Ontario Book Initiative; the Ontario Arts Council; the Canada Council for the Arts; and the Government of Canada, through the CBF, for our publishing activity.

Published in Canada by
Kids Can Press Ltd.
25 Dockside Drive
Toronto, ON M5A 0B5

Published in the U.S. by
Kids Can Press Ltd.
2250 Military Road
Tonawanda, NY 14150

www.kidscanpress.com

The artwork in this book was rendered in Photoshop.
The text is set in Minya Nouvelle.

Edited by Sheila Barry and Debbie Rogosin
Designed by Karen Powers

This book is smyth sewn casebound.
Manufactured in Malaysia, in 9/2012
by Tien Wah Press (Pte) Ltd.

CM 13 0 9 8 7 6 5 4 3 2 1

Library and Archives Canada Cataloguing in Publication

Fergus, Maureen

The day my mom came to kindergarten / written by Maureen Fergus ; illustrated by Mike Lowery.

ISBN 978-1-55453-698-6

I. Lowery, Mike, 1980– II. Title.

PS8611.E735D39 2013   jC813'.6   C2012-904552-7

Kids Can Press is a Corus™ Entertainment company

THE DAY MY MOM CAME TO KINDERGARTEN

MAUREEN FERGUS AND MIKE LOWERY

KIDS CAN PRESS

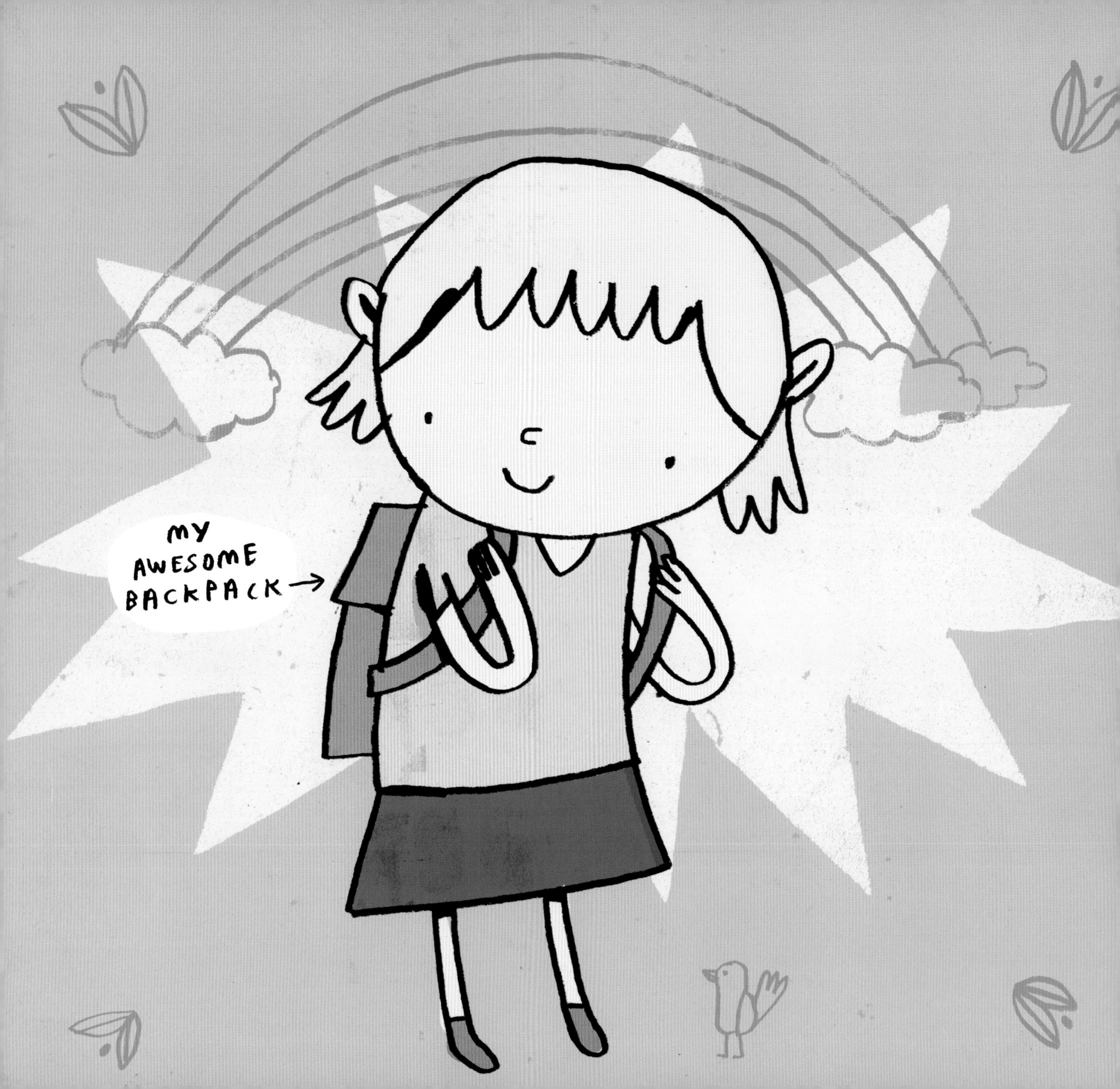
MY
AWESOME
BACKPACK

I *liked* KINDERGARTEN from the very 1ST day.

IT WAS BETTER THAN

a dinosaur museum

a circus

and a super-duper mega-three-scooper ice-cream sundae.

My mom was **HAPPY** for me, of course, but I got the feeling she was also a little **SAD** that I was growing up and starting to have adventures without her.

So one morning when I was standing in line outside the kindergarten door, instead of saying good-bye, I asked if she'd like to come inside.

BEEP BEEP!

She was so excited that she completely forgot her manners and tried to **BARGE** in at the front of the line.

"I'm sorry, Mom, but you need to go to the back of the line," I said. "Otherwise, it wouldn't be fair to the rest of us."

HEY!

HUH?!

Then, because I didn't want her to feel bad, I added,
"Don't worry. Everyone makes mistakes at first.
You'll be fine if you just watch me and do what I do."

She promised she would.

But I guess she forgot her promise because she walked right into the classroom without even taking off her outdoor shoes. My teacher, Ms. Beaudry, was nice about it. I was **SHOCKED**. Who did Mom think was going to clean up the muddy footprints she'd made on Ms. Beaudry's nice clean floor?

ZOOM

BOUNCE!

"**Mom**," I whispered, as we settled onto the carpet for our Letter of the Day activity, "school is nicer for everybody if you try to be considerate of others."

She promised she would make an effort.

But I guess she forgot that promise, too, because
the very next minute she **SHOUTED** out the answer
to Ms. Beaudry's question without raising her hand.

DINOSAUR!

GROAN!

I mashed my lips together to try to keep from making a groaning noise, and my face got so red that I pulled my whole head inside my shirt.

My mom looked down into my shirt, where my head was, and apologized for not waiting her turn to speak. I peeked up at her and pointed out that she wasn't paying attention to Ms. Beaudry.

"Talking while Ms. Beaudry is talking?" I whispered. "**VERY EMBARRASSING**, Mom."

It was hard to believe she'd ever been to kindergarten. She didn't even know the basics!

For the rest of the day it was one thing after another.

Mom remembered to take off her outdoor shoes after we visited the play structure, but **FORGOT** to put them neatly in her cubby.

She dropped crumbs **EVERYWHERE** during Snack Time
and tried to leave the table without cleaning them up.

When we were in the library, she kept forgetting to use her indoor voice, and she talked to me all through Story Time.

WHEEEE

She swung on the jungle ropes during gym class
when we were supposed to be playing beanbag tag.

During music class she went to the bathroom without asking permission and then **DAWDLED** so long on the way back that she missed her turn on the bongo drums.

And when she was having trouble with the scissors during Craft Time,
she made a loud huffy noise and **SLAMMED** them down on the table.

I was at my **WITS' END**. I didn't
know how Ms. Beaudry could stand it!

But Ms. Beaudry said I should remember that
Mom had never been to our class before.

"Sometimes it takes a while to get
comfortable with something new," she
reminded me with a smile. "Once your mom
gets used to the way we do things, I'm sure
she'll learn how to express her thoughts and
feelings in more appropriate ways."

We agreed that we should give Mom a little more time to figure things out. And I'm glad we did because **GUESS WHAT**? She got a lot better after that.

During Play Time she wanted to use the blocks to build a skyscraper, but because everyone else wanted to build a castle she agreed to help.

And later on, when the glue poured out too fast and ruined all the shapes she was trying to stick to the activity page, she didn't make a single huffy noise or slam the glue bottle down.

"I'm **PROUD** of how hard you tried today, Mom," I told her as we were getting ready to go home. "You can come back tomorrow if you want."

"Thank you, honey," she replied. "But I think it would be better if I only came back to visit once in a while. I can tell from the size of the chairs around here that kindergarten is meant for people much littler than me. And besides, kindergarten is **HARD WORK**!"

"That's true," I agreed. "But it's worth it."

"It sure is!" she said as she shoved her tissue paper craft into her purse. "Even so, I think I'll stick to working hard at something meant for people who sit on regular-sized chairs. You know — something that I'm already pretty good at."

I thought about this. Then I said, "You're **really** good at being a **mom**, Mom."

CRINKLE
RUMPLE

She said I was really good at being a kindergartener, crumpled some important notes from Ms. Beaudry into her pocket and gave me a **BIG HUG**.

As I hugged her back, I whispered, "Now, please take your place in line, Mom. Ms. Beaudry won't dismiss us until you do."